CW01582876

Published in 2024
by Two Windmills Limited

Marine House, Tide Mill Way
Woodbridge, Suffolk, IP12 1AP
United Kingdom

www.twowindmills.com

Written by Freddie Corrick
Illustrated by Mia Tivey

A CIP catalogue record for this book is available from the British Library.

Manufacturer's Representative: Eurolink Compliance Limited,
25 Herbert Place, Dublin, D02 AY86, Republic of Ireland
admin@eurolink-europe.ie

ISBN: 978-1-83555-107-3

Printed in Guangdong, China
10 9 8 7 6 5 4 3 2 1

MUMMY AND ME

Written by
Freddie Corrick

Illustrated by
Mia Tivey

Today is just for Mummy and me.
'What shall we do?' she asks, tickling my tummy.

'Breakfast first!'
I shout and bounce,
Then off the bed
I leap and pounce.

Mummy makes me my favourite food,
To match my happy, silly mood.

A dippy egg with soldiers on the side,
I eat it all up, my mouth open wide!

'Will you wear your pyjamas all day?
Let's get dressed to go out and play!'

I dress in an outfit that makes me smile,
My favourite hat is a green crocodile!

Mummy quickly grabs her things,
'Let's visit the park
and play on the swings!'

I slide and spin
and jump and run,
Playing in the park
is so much fun.

Soon I feel tired –
that's enough play.
'Let's go home,
we can shop on the way.'

We buy milk, bread
and strawberries too,
And I'm very patient in the queue.

When we get home, it's time for lunch,
Mummy makes something yummy to munch.

Then I help Mummy to tidy up,
I clean my plate and wash my cup.

Next, Mummy needs to wash the car,
'Let's make it shine as bright as a star!'

With bucket and sponge, and water to splash,
We clean up the car, quick as a flash.

Then Mummy and I
play with my toys,
Some are quiet
and some make NOISE!

We imagine, read, build and giggle.
We dance, stomp, whisper and wiggle.

There's a rumbling noise from my tummy,
We make dinner – it tastes super-yummy!

I help Mummy to add the cheese,
Then I eat it all up and say 'More, please!'

'What comes next?'
Mummy asks with a laugh.
'It must be time
for my bedtime bath!'

I pretend I'm a shark,
on the prowl,
Then I snuggle up
in a fluffy towel.

'I'm sleepy now,' I yawn with a sigh,
As we watch the moon shine in the sky.

Mummy reads a story and we sing a song,
And I know this is right where I belong.

'We had such a busy day!'
I tell my ted,
As Mummy tucks me
into my bed.

'Goodnight, my darling,'
she tickles my tummy.
I close my eyes, and say,
'Goodnight, Mummy.'